The Boy Who Could Fly

Sally Gardner is the author of *The Fairy Catalogue*, *The Glass Heart*, *A Book of Princesses* and other popular books for children, as well as the Magical Children series. She started out as a designer of sets and costumes for the theatre. She has a teenage son and twin daughters and lives in London.

ALSO BY SALLY GARDNER

The Invisible Boy
The Boy With the Magic Numbers
The Smallest Girl Ever
The Strongest Girl in the World
The Boy with the Lightning Feet

The Glass Heart
The Fairy Catalogue
Fairy Shopping
The Real Fairy Storybook (text by Georgie Adams)
A Book of Princesses
Playtime Rhymes
The Little Nut Tree

For older readers

I, Coriander

A Magical Children Book

The Boy Who Could Fly

Sally Gardner

Orion
Children's Books

For Dominic
with all my love

First published in Great Britain in 2001
by Dolphin Paperbacks
Reissued 2002 by Dolphin Paperbacks
an imprint of Orion Children's Books
a division of the Orion Publishing Group Ltd
Orion House
5 Upper St Martin's Lane,
London WC2H 9EA

7 9 10 8

Printed and bound in Great Britain by
Clays Ltd, St Ives plc

ISBN-13 978 1 85881 839 9

www.orionbooks.co.uk

1

Mrs Top opened her front door one grey Wednesday afternoon to find a Fat Fairy standing there.

"Is this 6 Valance Road, and are you Thomas Top's mother?" asked the Fat Fairy.

Mrs Top looked a little taken aback.

"Yes," she said, "but I think there must be some mistake. The birthday party has had to be cancelled."

The Fat Fairy adjusted her glasses and huffed.

"Well. I have got it written down here that I am booked for today, the fourth of May, at three o'clock for Thomas Top's ninth birthday," said the Fat Fairy firmly.

"And I never get it wrong."

"I don't understand. I didn't book anyone for Thomas's party. I mean, we always have Mr Spoons the magician. I never asked for a fairy," said Mrs Top.

"No one ever does, dear," said the Fat Fairy, "we are supposed to be a surprise."

Mrs Top was beginning to feel quite flustered.

"You see the party isn't happening today because Thomas is ill," she said. "We had to put it off. He's going to have it on the same day as his dad's birthday now."

"Well, that is nothing to do with me," said the Fat Fairy. "I am here just to wish him a happy birthday. It says nothing about entertainment or parties."

"Oh I see," said Mrs Top, feeling relieved, "you are some sort of singing telegram. I can't think who sent you."

"I wouldn't worry about it," said the Fat Fairy, smiling.

Thomas was propped up in bed. He felt terrible, with a sore throat and aching bones. A virus, the doctor had told his mum. He was to stay in bed until he felt better, and today was his birthday and he felt worse.

So far he had been given a book on fishing for beginners from his dad, a pen from his mum, a brown jumper from his Aunt Maud, and a pound stuck with masses of sticky tape to an old Christmas card from his Uncle Alfie. Things were not looking good when suddenly his mum entered the room, with the fattest fairy he had ever seen.

She had bright pink hair and was wearing a tutu two sizes too small. Her wings were lopsided and it looked as if she had sat on her tiara. If Thomas hadn't been feeling so unwell he would have burst out laughing.

"It's a surprise," said his mum anxiously.

The Fat Fairy looked around the room and huffed, then went and sat on the end of Thomas's bed.

"I wouldn't get too close to him," said Mum. "He could be infectious."

The Fat Fairy took no notice and said in a mournful voice, "Love a cup of tea, dear."

Mrs Top went downstairs, saying she wouldn't be a minute.

"Not much of a birthday," said the Fat Fairy, looking round Thomas's room and

at his presents.

"Why are you here?" said Thomas.

"To give you a birthday wish," said the Fat Fairy.

"You're joking, aren't you?" said Thomas.

"No," said the Fat Fairy. "Come on, just tell me what your wish is, and then I can be on my way."

"I don't know," said Thomas. He wasn't sure what to make of her. "This is just a game, isn't it?"

"It's no game," said the Fat Fairy. "Come on, let's get this finished with before your mum comes back with tea and fairy cakes."

"I wish I was..." said Thomas.

"No good," interrupted the Fat Fairy. "You can't wish for all the money in the world or to turn Aunt Maud into a sheep. It just won't work like that. You have to wish for something like having the most beautiful hair or being able to sing like a cherub, or being a whizz at computers. Now do you get it?"

Thomas looked at her again. "Mum doesn't have any fairy cakes," he said.

The fairy shrugged her wings. "Come on, come on," she said. "Concentrate, it's not every day you get a wish granted."

"You're kidding, right?" said Thomas.

"Whatever," said the Fat Fairy. "Just get on with it."

"I wish that..." said Thomas.

"No good," the fairy interrupted. "You

can't wish for your father to be fun. It has to do with you, Thomas," she said gently. "After all, today is your ninth birthday."

Thomas looked surprised. "How did you know I was going to wish for that?" he said.

"Quick," said the Fat Fairy as Mum's footsteps could be heard coming up the stairs.

Thomas said the first thing that came into his head. "I wish I could fly." Why he said that he couldn't think.

"Nice one," said the Fat Fairy, standing up just as Mum entered the room with two cups of tea and a plate of fairy cakes.

"I'm all done and dusted, dear," said the Fat Fairy, giving a loud belch. "All this wishing plays havoc with my insides," she went on, gulping down the tea and putting three fairy cakes in her handbag. "Well, I can't stay here all day enjoying myself."

And without so much as a goodbye,

she made her way down
the stairs. Mum followed,
saying, "Wait a minute, I
was wondering which
company sent you," but by
the time she had made it to
the front door the Fat Fairy
had vanished.

2

Thomas went back to school the following Monday.

Monday was his worst day. There were games and Thomas hated games. "Could I have a note saying that I've been ill?" he asked his mum.

"No," said his dad firmly. "If you are well enough to go back to school, young man, you are well enough to play games."

"I think, Alan, that's a bit hard," said his mum. "He has been very unwell."

"I am not having that boy mummy-coddled any more," said Dad firmly. "We have had quite enough interruption to our routine."

So Thomas stood in the hell zone that was gym. Miss Peach took no nonsense from her class. She had all the apparatus out in the school hall: the beam, the trampoline, the mats, the dreaded jumping horse.

All the class lined up ready to jump over the horse. It usually went with a good rhythm, that is until it came to Thomas's turn. Today would be no different, he thought miserably.

Thomas closed his eyes and started his run, waiting for the bump as he hit the horse, the shout that would be Miss Peach telling him he wasn't trying hard enough, and the laughter that would be his classmates.

Except he didn't hit the horse, and all
he heard was a loud gasp. When he
opened his eyes he was amazed to
find he was about six feet off
the ground.

Thomas landed
ungracefully on the
other side of the horse.

"Thomas Top, what do you think you're doing?" said a shocked Miss Peach.

"Nothing, miss," said Thomas, "just jumping."

The class was silent. Children can jump high, but six feet off the ground was unbelievable by anyone's standards. Miss Peach was seeing things, that was it. She clapped her hands. "Now everyone, settle down and let's do it one more time. Well done, Thomas, for getting over the horse."

It happened again. This time Thomas found himself about eight feet off the ground and heading for the other side of the school hall. He landed with a loud bump.

"That's it, Thomas Top. I will not have this kind of showing-off in my lesson," said Miss Peach. "You will go and sit outside until you calm down."

Thomas sat outside in the draughty corridor in his plimsolls and a flimsy white T-shirt and brown shorts.

"What are you doing out here, Thomas Top?" said Mr March the headmaster.

"I got sent out for showing off," said Thomas apologetically.

Mr March laughed. "Not like you, Top, you're always such a quiet little chap. Come on, let's see what all this is about."

The class were now on the trampoline.

"Sorry to interrupt you, Miss Peach, but this little fellow tells me he's been sent outside for showing off, is that right?"

"Yes," said Miss Peach flatly. "He was jumping too high."

Mr March looked puzzled. "Jumping too high? Well, I never would have thought he had it in him."

"Neither would I," said Miss Peach, who did not appreciate the headmaster's interruption one little bit.

"Well," said Mr March, "I'm sure Thomas will behave himself now, and perhaps he can join in on the trampoline."

Thomas had always hated the trampoline. He was no good at coordination; jumping up and down terrified the socks off him. He climbed up gingerly, his face pale.

"Don't forget to bend your knees," said Miss Peach sternly.

Thomas bent his knees and straightened up again, feeling very wobbly on his feet.

"He's not really trying, miss," said Suzi Morris.

"He didn't jump," said Joe Corry, another boy in his class. "He just bent his knees."

"Now come on," said Mr March. "I'm sure you can do better than that. Let's see you jumping nice and high."

What happened next gave Thomas the biggest shock of his life. He found himself going up and up towards the ceiling of the school hall, his legs and arms waving about before grabbing hold of a beam and hanging there.

Thomas was scared
of heights. They made
him feel sick. He was now
higher than he had ever
been in his life and he didn't
know how it had happened.

"Help, please!" cried Thomas.

"Oh my word," cried Mr
March. "Get a ladder, quick!
Hold on boy, we'll get you
down."

But it was too
late. Thomas felt his
fingers getting weak.
There was no
way he was
going to
survive this.

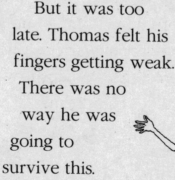

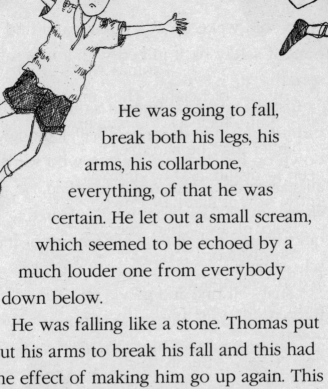

He was going to fall,
break both his legs, his
arms, his collarbone,
everything, of that he was
certain. He let out a small scream,
which seemed to be echoed by a
much louder one from everybody
down below.

He was falling like a stone. Thomas put
out his arms to break his fall and this had
the effect of making him go up again. This
couldn't be happening. He felt he was on
a rollercoaster. Perhaps it was all a
bad dream.

He would wake up in a minute and find himself safely back in bed with a nice safe sore throat.

Instead he found himself sitting on a beam high up in the school hall, looking down on his class and teacher who were all staring up at him, open-mouthed. He clung on for dear life while Mr March quickly ushered all the children out of the school hall.

"That's all fine and good," said Miss Peach to herself, "but the question is how are we going to get him down?"

3

Mrs Top arrived at the school in a terrible state. "What kind of incident? Why have I been called here?" she said. "I have already had to take a week off work with Thomas being ill."

Mr March looked quite embarrassed.

Thomas felt miserable. It had taken over an hour to get him down. In the end Miss Peach had had to climb up and with a lot of gentle talking, which didn't come easy to her, she had managed to persuade a very shaky Thomas to make his way to the floor.

"Well," said Mr March, clearing his throat, "Thomas jumped."

"Isn't he supposed to jump, isn't that what they do in gym, jump?" said Mrs Top.

"Yes," said Mr March. "Not quite this kind of jumping though."

"I'm sorry, you've lost me," said Mrs Top, looking even more baffled.

The headmaster coughed. "Please sit down."

Mrs Top perched on the edge of her chair while the headmaster told her, using a lot of pauses and erms, what had happened in the school hall. He had to admit that it sounded rather far-fetched.

When Mrs Top had heard what the headmaster had to say, she stood up. "You have brought me all the way to school because Thomas jumped," she said.

"I am sorry, but I don't understand what you are talking about, Mr March. All I know is I should never have let him play games, after he's been so poorly."

"Thomas," said Mr March, "will you please jump."

Thomas looked at his mum.

"Do I have to?" he asked her.

"Yes, let's get this over with," said Mum wearily. "Then I can get back to work."

Thomas bent his knees and pretended to jump, keeping his feet fixed on the floor.

"There," said Mrs Top. "There's nothing wrong with that. He's never been all that good at sports."

"Thomas," said the headmaster firmly. "I would like you to do a proper jump, not a pretend one."

Thomas looked from his mum's face to Mr March and knew there was no way out. He closed his eyes and jumped.

He hit his head so hard on the ceiling

that a bit of plaster fell onto the carpet below. Thomas landed with a thud as Mrs Top fainted. She recovered to find the school nurse holding her hand and Mr March pouring a cup of sweet tea. Mrs Top felt flustered by all the attention and stood up, feeling weak.

"I think you should sit down until you get over the shock," said the nurse kindly.

"There is nothing to get over," said Mum, getting up and adjusting her coat. "We are just ordinary people and jumping very high doesn't run in the family."

"Quite so, Mrs Top," said the headmaster. "All the same, perhaps Thomas should spend a few more days at home until he is quite better."

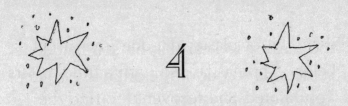

4

There was no way Mrs Top would be going back to work today. She took Thomas's hand and they left the school and walked home. She looked pale and worried.

"We won't have to tell Dad, will we?" said Thomas nervously.

"I am afraid we will," said Mrs Top. "He would get to hear about it sooner or later."

Thomas knew this would be the worst part. His dad prided himself on their being just an ordinary family. They lived in a three-bedroomed house that looked no different from any of the other three-bedroomed houses in their street. Mr Top had a regular job as a button salesman, and Mrs Top worked in an office. They were ordinary people. Nothing extraordinary ever happened to them and that was the way Mr Top liked it. His dad would not be too pleased to hear that his son had done something so out of the ordinary as jump as high as the ceiling.

That evening Mum told Dad what had happened at school. When Mum had finished Thomas gave a demonstration.

His dad smiled and said, "Rita my dear, boys don't jump to the top of school halls or hit their heads on kitchen ceilings. It is simply not possible for anybody to jump that high. I think this is a classic case of people letting their imaginations get the better of them." He laughed. "Perhaps, young man," he said, looking at Thomas's worried face, "April Fool's day has come late this year."

Thomas felt relieved. It wasn't exactly

what he thought his dad
would say. He had
imagined he was going to
be in big trouble.

"But Alan," said Mum,
"you must have seen him jump
just now. Thomas, do it again."

Thomas did as he was told.

"There you see," said Mum, "that
can't be normal."

"Rita, this is the last time I'll say it. Boys
don't jump that high," said Dad, beginning
to lose his temper. "I don't know what's
come over you, Rita. You will be giving
the boy all sorts of stupid ideas."

Thomas couldn't believe it. Surely his
dad could see him jumping up to the
ceiling? Mum was right, he shouldn't be
able to do that.

"I think," said Dad sternly, "that Thomas
just needs an early night. Then he will be
as right as rain."

There was a terrible silence, then Mum smiled weakly. There seemed little point in arguing. "Perhaps you're right," she said. "It is all a bit odd."

"Of course I'm right," said Dad. "I am always right. Now, we will hear no more on the subject. There's nothing wrong with Thomas. He is just an ordinary little boy. There's definitely no excuse for missing any more school. I will speak to Mr March tomorrow and put an end to all this nonsense."

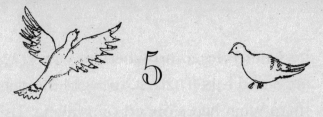

5

Thomas sat in bed that evening thinking fairies weren't fat, were they? All the fairies he had ever seen in fairy books were thin with beautiful long hair and wings that twinkled. They weren't fat and they didn't belch. It was hard to believe she was a real fairy and if she was, had she the power to make a wish come true? But then how did the fairy know what his real wish would be, or about Mum and the fairy cakes? He lay in bed looking at the stars that shone bright in the night sky, and thought about all that had happened that day.

Suddenly Thomas felt as if a light bulb had gone on in his head. He remembered that he'd wished he could fly. He got out of bed and gingerly stood on his duvet cover. He wasn't quite sure what to do. Then he thought back to the school hall;

he seemed to go up when he waved his arms and legs. That's it, thought Thomas, that's what had stopped him falling. This time he pretended he was swimming. He felt a bit silly doing a sort of hopeless breast stroke in the air. Except it wasn't silly at all. He was now way above the bed, flying around the room.

Thomas could feel the excitement from the tips of his toes to the top of his head. He felt it like a delicious feeling of melted chocolate. Thomas Top, nine years old, Thomas Top could fly.

6

The next day Mr Top took Thomas into school and spoke to the headmaster while Thomas waited in the corridor. Mr Top came out and so did Mr March. "Glad we were able to sort out that little misunderstanding," said Mr Top.

Mr March also seemed relieved. "Now I have had a night to sleep on it," he said, "I think you are right." He looked at Thomas. What were they all thinking of? Of course this boy couldn't jump that high, it was impossible! Really, this had all got out of hand. He was running a busy school, not a circus.

"We can safely put the whole incident down to an over-active imagination," said Mr March, "least said, soonest mended."

"Quite so," said Dad.

That was the end of it, as far as the

staff were concerned. His teacher Miss Peach, who had never allowed herself the luxury of imagination, was only too delighted to agree with the headmaster. It must have been the stresses and strains of teaching that made them think that such an unremarkable boy as Thomas Top could jump that high. Thomas hadn't done anything extraordinary. He never had and he never would. He was just your average child, nothing out of the ordinary.

Except his classmates didn't see it that way, and stories of Thomas's incredible jump quickly spread round the school.

At break that day Neil, the biggest boy in junior school and a bully to boot, came over to where Thomas and his friends were playing.

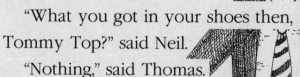

"What you got in your shoes then, Tommy Top?" said Neil.

"Nothing," said Thomas.

Shoes were a very sore point with Thomas. He would have loved to have trainers like everyone else in his class, but his dad insisted he wore sensible ordinary brown lace-ups.

"Nothing," said Thomas again.

Neil didn't look convinced. "Well, that's not what I heard. What I heard is you jumped and hit the roof of the school hall."

"Everybody just imagined it," said Thomas.

"I don't think so," said Neil. "Come on baby, Tommy Top, show us what you got."

Thomas paused. As no grown-up believed he could jump that high, he had nothing to lose by showing the school bully that he could not only jump but fly.

"Go on then," said Neil, "bet you can't, Tommy Top, bet you can't."

Thomas started doing his swimming strokes.

Neil burst out laughing and so did the other kids who had gathered around to see what was going on.

"Oh diddums," said Neil, "what are you..." He didn't finish what he was saying because Thomas was now flying upwards. He was a little bit wobbly. It felt strange not having any walls or ceilings to stop him from going higher, and also a lot more scary. Thomas was rather pleased when he came down and landed safely on the ground.

"Miss, miss," shouted a little girl who was standing next to Miss Peach, "look, Thomas Top is flying!"

"It must be fun to have an imagination and be able to see things that aren't there," said Miss Peach.

Neil was quite lost for words when Thomas landed.

"I would shut your mouth before you swallow a fly," said Thomas, smiling. It felt very good to see all his classmates look so amazed, as if he had just landed from the moon.

A near riot had broken out in the playground. It took Miss Peach quite some time to get the children into class.

"Now settle down, children," said Miss Peach. "I don't want to hear any more stories about jumping or flying. Will you open your maths books at page three."

After school finished the whole class had said they would like to come to Thomas's birthday when he had it. This in itself was quite something. Usually nobody wanted to come to Thomas's parties because of Mr Spoons the magician, who did the same old magic tricks year after year. But Dad wouldn't hear of having anybody else. "We've always had Mr Spoons since you were five years old. It wouldn't be your party without him."

It was not surprising that no one wanted to come, especially not when Suzi Morris had her party on or round the same day. Last year she had had Aunt Hat

and her Magic Handbag, and she had
become the most popular girl in the
school overnight. Everyone wanted to go
to Suzi's party. In the end she had only
handed out invitations to those who had
promised to bring the biggest and best
presents. There had hardly been anyone at
Thomas's party. But this year it was going
to be different.

7

As the week went on Thomas's flying got better and he became braver and bolder. He even had the cheek to fly up on the school playing field and get a football that had been kicked high up in a tree, which had gone down well with his mates and unnoticed by his games teacher. So far no grown-up had noticed him flying.

His most daring venture so far was to go to the corner shop and get some bread for Mum. Thomas had started walking. Then he wondered, as nobody was about, whether he could fly. It would be quicker and he could test if he really was invisible while flying. There was only one woman out walking her dog and Thomas wondered if she would let out a scream when she saw him fly past. She didn't, though the dog barked wildly. Oh well, he thought, if no one can see me then I might go a little bit higher.

He flew right up to the top of a building and sat there seeing the world in quite a different way, watching the sunlight play over the rooftops. He was no longer afraid of heights.

Then Thomas realised to his alarm that he wasn't alone. Sitting a little way off was a man in paint overalls who was looking straight at him. Thomas felt a moment of panic. He only hoped that he was invisible to this man as he seemed to be to everyone else.

"The Fat Fairy, I take it," said the man. Thomas nodded, hardly believing what he was hearing.

"How did you know?"

"Oh, I know all about the Fat Fairy. I saw you flying round your garden the other day," said the man, with a huge smile on his face. "May I introduce myself?

I am Mr Vinnie, at your service."

"You can fly too," said Thomas in disbelief.

"How else do you think I got up here?" said Mr Vinnie, laughing at Thomas's surprised face. "Why did you think you were the only person who could fly?"

Thomas shrugged his shoulders. "I didn't think about it."

"What's your name, lad?" said Mr Vinnie kindly.

"Thomas Top," said Thomas.

"Nice to meet you," said Mr Vinnie. "When I was a whipper-snapper of your age the Fat Fairy gave me a birthday wish too, and like you I wished that I could fly.

I didn't know it at the time, but it was the best thing I ever could have wished for."

"It hasn't gone away, then," said Thomas.

Mr Vinnie laughed. "No it hasn't gone away," he said. "I have been flying nearly all my life."

"I didn't think it would last," said Thomas. "I was wondering if one day I would fall tumble to the ground."

"Isn't that funny. I remember thinking exactly the same thing when I was your age. Then I met other boys and girls who could fly and that was great fun. We grew up in the air, so to speak. We've all gone our different ways, but we still keep in touch."

"So there are others as well," said Thomas. He found this a very comforting thought, though he couldn't quite think why.

"Yes, scattered all over the place," said Mr Vinnie.

"And no one noticed you flying? Are you invisible like me?" asked Thomas.

Mr Vinnie's face creased with laughter. "You are not invisible, Thomas. Neither am I, though I am more invisible than you because I am old and people don't take any notice of us old wrinklies at the best of times, let alone when we fly," said Mr Vinnie. "No, Thomas, it's simple. Humans don't fly, so no one sees us." With that Mr

Vinnie flew up into the air and turned a somersault before neatly landing on top of a pigeon, who did not like having his feathers ruffled by such a large bird.

"Wow," said Thomas. "How did you do that?"

"I've been at this a long time," said Mr Vinnie. "Now show me what you can do, Thomas."

So Thomas did his swimming strokes.

Mr Vinnie watched. "It looks exhausting. Don't you get tired?"

"Yes," said Thomas, "but I don't know what else to do."

"You don't need to wave anything about. You just have to trust that you

can fly. A wish is a wish and it stays with you for ever," said Mr Vinnie.

Mr Vinnie showed him how he could fly without moving his arms or legs. It looked so beautiful, as if he had control over the wind and the air.

Up on the top of a building near the corner shop, while the sun was setting, Mr Vinnie told Thomas all he knew about flying. Thomas flew home in great excitement.

Mum was very cross. "Where have you been and what have you been doing and where is the bread?" she said.

"I'm sorry. I forgot it," said Thomas. He hadn't meant to. It was just the thrill of flying and meeting Mr Vinnie. It was no good saying all that to his mum. She wouldn't understand.

"Oh," said she, "head in the clouds, I suppose."

"Yes, Mum," said Thomas.

8

At first the magic of flying was so wonderful it hadn't really mattered tuppence that no grown-up was aware of what an incredible thing he could do. In fact it had been very useful. It had given him a freedom which otherwise would have made learning to fly impossible. As he got better, he began to feel more sad that his mum still couldn't see what he could do. His dad had said nothing, even when he had sat in the garden watching Thomas do somersaults in the air. It felt disappointing that neither his mum or dad could see just how good he was.

As the evenings got lighter Mr Vinnie and Thomas would meet in the park where they could fly properly without buildings to get in the way.

Mr Vinnie said that it was sad that so

many people walked with their heads
bowed down, looking out for dog poo, and
not seeing the magic that was all around
them. The more Thomas flew the more he
thought how wonderful everything was
and how being so high up with the birds
made you see the world in a different way.

Mr Vinnie told Thomas about his dad
and how when he was young he had
wanted him to get a proper job, like being
a banker. "But once you have flown up

where the sky is blue," said Mr Vinnie, "you couldn't be tied down to a desk imprisoned in four walls." So he had become a painter and decorator, which was just the ticket. He could work faster than anyone else in the business. Flying up and down meant there was no need for ladders and he could float on his back to paint ceilings.

Thomas found that he could talk to Mr Vinnie in a way that he had never been able to talk to his dad.

"Do you have any children?" Thomas asked Mr Vinnie as they sat one evening at the top of Alexandra Palace, watching the sun setting over London, turning it from red to gold.

"No," said Mr Vinnie sadly. "Annie, my dear wife, and me wanted kids but they didn't happen." Mr Vinnie smiled. "I am not complaining, Annie and me had a wonderful life together." He had often

taken his wife flying. She couldn't fly, but
Mr Vinnie was a strong man and, as he
told Thomas, his wife was as light as a
sparrow. Sadly she had died last year and
Mr Vinnie said he thought he would
never fly again. But then one day he had
seen Thomas flying in his garden and he
felt that he couldn't give up, not when
there was so much magic in the world.

"I'm sorry," said Thomas.

"No need, Thomas, but thank you," said
Mr Vinnie. "Annie would have been right
chuffed to have met you."

9

It is hard to imagine your parents being young and when Thomas thought about his dad he couldn't see his dad as a child ever really laughing and enjoying himself. Dad was more interested in Thomas doing well in maths and things like that.

"There's no money to be made in having fun," said Dad. "To get a proper job you need maths." Maths, Dad told him, is the cornerstone of your future. But Thomas was no good at maths, whereas flying was something he could do perfectly. Dad, thought Thomas gloomily, could suck all the fun out of a day without trying. It was like their dreaded fishing trips.

Fishing was Dad's one little hobby. He bought every magazine and book on the subject. He prided himself on having the

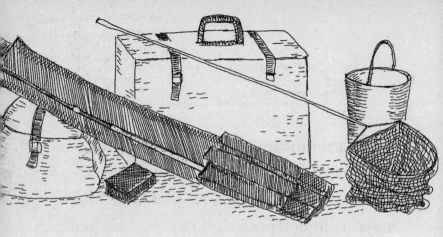

latest fishing rod and the most up-to-date
equipment. There was nothing Dad didn't
know about fishing except how to catch a
fish.

He would pack the car very carefully
on Saturday morning,
bright and early, making
sure nothing was left out.
It took ages and if Dad
couldn't find this or that
they would have to stop
everything until it was
found. By the time they set off
it was no longer bright, because Mum and
Dad would have had an argument, and it

was no longer early.

The reservoir was a dreary place that backed on to the local gasworks. This was where Dad liked to go fishing. They would arrive so late that all the good fishing spots would have gone. It hardly seemed worth all the effort, because in the end there wasn't that much time left to catch a fish. They would both come home tired and fed up and Thomas would wait for the awful words, "We'll get it right next time, son." His dad always said it and they never did.

There was no doubt that Dad worked hard. Except for Saturday's fishing trips he would spend the weekends studying his button sale figures. Mum would sit alone at the kitchen table looking through magazines and dreaming of what her house would look like if only she could paint it the way she wanted. Dad had painted it magnolia and brown when they first moved in. Nothing out of the ordinary, and that was the way he liked it.

A sadness now seemed to hang in the air like a mist. It had definitely got worse since Thomas had taken up flying. Dad had become more rigid, seeing less and less of what was around him. At times Thomas felt sorry that the Fat Fairy had been unable to give him his first wish that his dad could have fun. Then maybe everything would have been all right.

10

School was much better than it had ever been. Thomas had gone from being unnoticed, with only one friend, a boy called Spud, to being one of the most popular boys in the school. This was in no small measure helped by the fact that teachers couldn't or wouldn't see what Thomas could do. It gave him an edge over all the grown-ups, and a feeling of power which also frightened him.

His friends, like Spud, found it hard to believe that Miss Peach, who had seen Thomas jump and hit the beams in the gym, could not now see him fly. It seemed unfair to Thomas that his teachers would get cross with him for not being any good at games. For playing football as if he had four left feet while not seeing that he was amazing, a star. In the air, Thomas had a beauty and a

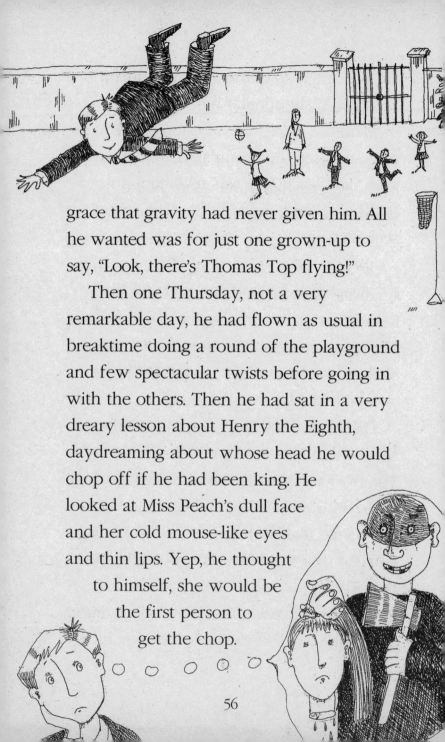

grace that gravity had never given him. All he wanted was for just one grown-up to say, "Look, there's Thomas Top flying!"

Then one Thursday, not a very remarkable day, he had flown as usual in breaktime doing a round of the playground and few spectacular twists before going in with the others. Then he had sat in a very dreary lesson about Henry the Eighth, daydreaming about whose head he would chop off if he had been king. He looked at Miss Peach's dull face and her cold mouse-like eyes and thin lips. Yep, he thought to himself, she would be the first person to get the chop.

He was interrupted from his daydream by Miss Peach shouting at him.

"Thomas Top, are you listening? You are to go and see the headmaster immediately," said Miss Peach. She was reading a note that had been handed her by the school secretary.

"Why?" asked Thomas.

Miss Peach looked very red and blotchy. "Thomas, just do what you are told without talking back at me, and take your coat and rucksack with you," she said angrily.

This wasn't a good sign.

Sitting in the headmaster's office was his mum. She had been crying. Thomas felt he must have done something very bad, but he wasn't sure what.

"I'm sorry, Mrs Top," Mr March was saying, "but we can't cater for a child who is disruptive."

Thomas couldn't believe what he was hearing.

"I therefore think a suspension is the only course of action open to us, and we can review the case after the board of governors have had their meeting."

Mrs Top said nothing but took Thomas's hand and they walked home in complete silence. Thomas knew his dad would not be pleased. He would be grounded for weeks – maybe years. His party would be cancelled, he thought miserably and that would be a shame, especially when there were so many coming.

"It's not fair, Mum," said Thomas when they got home. "I didn't do anything wrong. I just flew round the playground and got balls out of trees, that sort of thing. I wasn't naughty or anything like that. And everybody liked it and now all my class want to come to my party and I won't be able to have it."

Mum sat at the kitchen table, her head in her hands.

"Mum," said Thomas, "all I want is for someone to see that I can fly and that I'm not making it up. I haven't been disruptive, whatever that means."

Mum looked out of the window at the birds flying past and said almost in a whisper, "I know, Thomas. I've seen you out there flying and in my heart I am so proud of you. But what could I say when your dad and all your teachers refuse to see it?"

Thomas put his arms round his mum's neck. "I'm sorry. I didn't mean to upset you."

"Oh, I know you didn't. It's not your fault, Thomas. What I would give to have wings like you and be able to fly!" said Mum.

"I don't have wings," said Thomas.

"I know," said Mum, "and you're right, you can do something so wonderful and magical that it fills me with envy. What is it like up there?"

"Pretty good, really good. People don't notice you. Only children and dogs stare. I have even flown up the High Street with my friend, Mr Vinnie," said Thomas proudly.

"Who is Mr Vinnie?" said Mum.

"He's a painter and decorator who has got his bus pass. He doesn't use it because like me he can fly. There are quite a few, Mr Vinnie says, but I have only met him. There's not so many children now because they don't wish for it any more."

"Why not?" said Mum.

"They wish for things like beauty and brains and long hair and to be the cleverest computer whizz in the world. It's getting rare, Mr Vinnie says, for children to wish for simple things like flying," said Thomas.

"I see," said Mum, who was seeing Thomas with new eyes. This was her son, her little baby, this incredible boy who knew all about flying! "Well, I think we should invite Mr Vinnie round for tea. I would very much like to meet him," said Mum, smiling. "Would you like to ring him and see if he can come next Tuesday?"

"But what about Dad?" said Thomas.

11

That night there was a terrible row in the house. Thomas had never seen his dad quite so cross. He wouldn't hear a word Mum had to say. "Are you mad, Rita?" he shouted. "Boys don't fly."

Thomas's party was cancelled.

Dad phoned up Mr Spoons, who said he was sorry to hear that, but pleased to know that boys these days did still get punished for being bad.

"He hasn't been bad," said Mum desperately, "he has only been flying."

"Will you put a sock in it once and for all with all this flying nonsense," yelled Dad, going blue in the face. "We are an ordinary family. Flying is for fairy tales."

"I can't take much more of this, Alan," sobbed Mum.

Thomas went to bed with tears running

down his face. He could hear Mum and
dad in the kitchen shouting at one
another, even when he pulled his duvet
right up over his head.

   The next morning things were not
much better. Dad didn't say a word during
breakfast and left for work still not
speaking. Mum had to phone the office
where she worked to say she wouldn't be
coming in for a week, or until she could
get some childcare sorted out. "I'm going

to lose that job if I have to take any more time off," she said to the kitchen wall.

"I'm sorry," said Thomas, who had just come in and was standing behind her, tears pricking his eyes. Mum turned and smiled.

"It's not your fault. Come on, don't look so sad," she said. "It's just hard being grown-up. Sometimes we fail to see the magic in the world, and that's our problem, not yours."

Things didn't get any better over the weekend. Although it was sunny outside it felt like winter in the house. Dad was only speaking in yes's and no's. He went fishing by himself after making a dreadful fuss about a fishing hat that he couldn't find.

Mum had let Thomas have Spud over to play while Dad was out. They spent their time behind the back of the garden shed.

"What's in there?" Spud asked.

"I don't know. Dad doesn't let me go in. He says it's just for the lawnmower," said Thomas, kicking a stone.

The boys talked about Thomas's party and what a bad thing it was that it had been cancelled, especially when it had been the most talked-about party in the school for ages.

"Well," said Thomas, "in a way I'm quite pleased it's not happening. Can you see everybody sitting there and watching Mr Spoons' magic show for babies?"

"You would have to do a lot of flying to make up for that," said Spud.

On one thing they both agreed, the school was wrong to have suspended Thomas for just being amazing at flying.

"It's not on the National Curriculum, more's the pity," said Spud.

"Hey, wouldn't it be well wicked if Miss Peach had to give lessons in flying," said Thomas.

"I think," said Spud, "the teachers at our school are the living dead."

Thomas laughed. It felt good to be outside with your best mate and the sun shining. Thomas soared up in

the air and down again,
Spud running after him. It
looked as if Spud was chasing
a kite shaped like a boy. On
the last run round the garden
Spud hit the door of the
garden shed by mistake and
to his surprise it opened.
Thomas landed next to him
and they pushed the door
a little farther open.

"We shouldn't go in," said
Thomas. "Dad would
explode if he found
we'd been snooping."

"There's something behind the lawnmower," said Spud.

Thomas looked again, his eyes getting used to the gloom of the shed. Spud was right. Whatever it was was well hidden, with a large tarpaulin covering it.

"Go on," said Spud. "I'll keep a lookout."

Thomas hesitated in the doorway. But his curiosity got the better of him and he squeezed in carefully so as not to disturb anything. He lifted up the cover gingerly and looked underneath.

What Thomas was expecting he didn't really know, but he was amazed by what

he saw: a beautiful old motorbike with a sidecar, its chrome shining like star dust. It looked almost new. The boys stood open-mouthed, looking at it.

"Do you think your dad stole it?" asked Spud.

"No," said Thomas, "Dad would never do anything like that."

Still, he had to agree with Spud that it was a bit odd Dad having such a great motorbike hidden in the garden shed. They quickly put the covers back and made sure the bolt was properly fastened this time.

Mum brought them out some lemonade and biscuits, saying Spud should go home soon. The boys sat eating on the grass.

"A mystery," said Spud. "Perhaps your dad has another life that you don't know about."

Thomas didn't think so. He couldn't see his dad ever having that much fun.

12

It seemed to take forever for Tuesday to come round. Why is it, wondered Thomas, that the things you look forward to seem to take so long, and then when they come, seem to go so fast? But at last Mr Vinnie arrived, looking very smart. He was wearing an old flying jacket.

Mum had put the tea out in the garden on a table laid with a white linen tablecloth and a bunch of flowers. Thomas had helped her make a cake. He had great fun putting in the strawberry jam and whipped cream. It looked a picture.

Mum and Mr Vinnie got on very well and she asked him all the questions that Thomas thought a non-flying grown-up might ask. Like, is it safe? Will Thomas hurt himself? Could the wind carry him away? Should he only go flying when it's

sunny? Mr Vinnie ate the cake, which he said was delicious, and assured Mum that Thomas was doing very well and there was no need to worry.

"Would you like to see what flying is like, Rita?" said Mr Vinnie.

"You mean fly up there? It's not possible," said Mum, blushing.

"Oh yes it is Mum, it is. Tell her, Mr Vinnie, tell her," said Thomas in great excitement.

Mr Vinnie told her about Annie his
wife who was a non-flyer like herself, and
how they had flown together.

"You used to fly to France, didn't you,"
said Thomas, who now couldn't wait to
show his mum what it was like.

Mum stood in the middle of the garden.
Mr Vinnie took one hand and Thomas
held the other.

"What do I do now?" said Mum, feeling
rather foolish.

"Nothing at all, just hold on to us and don't let go."

No sooner had Mr Vinnie said this than Mum realised she was way up above the ground, looking down on the little gardens and houses that lay like a patchwork quilt beneath her.

"Oh, this is wonderful!" she cried. "Oh, this is magic!"

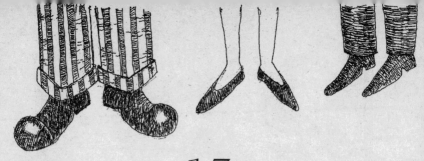

13

"What do you think you're doing, Rita?" shouted Dad as Mum landed back in the garden.

"Flying," said Mum proudly.

"And who is this man and what is he doing here?" said Dad. He did not look at all happy. Mum tried to explain and so did Thomas and Mr Vinnie. Dad was having none of it.

"I've had enough of this madness. What has come over you, Rita?"

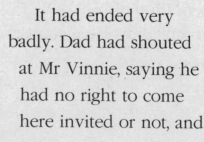

It had ended very badly. Dad had shouted at Mr Vinnie, saying he had no right to come here invited or not, and

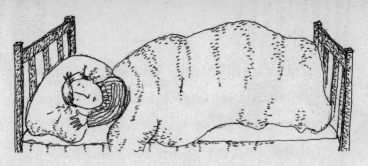

he was going to hold Mr Vinnie
personally responsible for all this flying
nonsense. Thomas was sent to bed early
and once again he could hear his parents
arguing downstairs.

The next morning he found Mum
sitting alone at the kitchen table. Her face
had a sad upside-down look about it. Dad
had already left for work.

"Why is Dad so cross?" Thomas asked
her as he was eating a bowl of Wheetos.
Mum looked out of the window and up at
the pale blue sky.

"I think it's Dad's work that makes him
so unhappy. He is most probably a bit like
you, bullied at work by his boss for not
getting the right amount of button sales."

"I'm not bullied any more," said Thomas.

"I know," said Mum. "It doesn't work being ordinary. Being ordinary is harder for some than being extraordinary."

"I think you are right," said Thomas.

Mum made a cup of tea and told Thomas what his dad had been like when she had first met him. He was so different from the other young men she knew, and that was what she loved about him. He was out of the ordinary. Like his motorbike, which had a sidecar and a name like a movie star – Harley Davidson.

"What happened to the motorbike, Mum?" asked Thomas. He didn't want to tell her he'd seen it.

"Oh, it's in the garden shed," said Mum. "But do you know, Thomas, your dad used to be a whizz at magic tricks? He could make flowers come out of his hat and coins from behind his ears."

"What happened?" said Thomas. "Why isn't he like that now?"

"Dad wanted so much for you. He was going to make our fortunes. We were all going to live in a grand house. Dad was going to be king of the button sales, except it didn't quite work out that way," said Mum sadly. "He thought he had to be grown-up and responsible, and he just got stuck. Time that goes so slowly for you just flew past for us. We lost our dreams. Anyway, Dad thought dreams were for kids."

Thomas thought, well, that explains the mystery of the motorbike. How odd, he thought, to own such a wonderful machine and keep it hidden in the garden shed. It was not all his dad had kept hidden, Thomas thought miserably.

14

Thomas knew it was bad. His mum had gone to stay with her sister and she wasn't back. Today was Saturday, his dad's birthday, and he should have been having his party. He lay in bed wondering what was going to happen. He had made Dad a card and a little present, a painted box for his fish hooks. He was about to get out of bed and give them to him when the front doorbell rang and he heard a familiar voice. He got out of bed and ran downstairs in his dressing-gown, forgetting his slippers. His dad was standing in the doorway.

"I don't know what you want," he was saying. In front of him stood the Fat Fairy.

"It's quite simple, Mr Top. You are Alan Top, Thomas's dad?" said the Fat Fairy.

"Yes," said Dad.

"I am here to give you a wish."

"Is this some kind of practical joke?" said Dad. "Because if it is I am not in the mood."

"No," said the Fat Fairy.

"Dad," said Thomas, pulling at his sleeve.

"Thomas, not now," his dad said sharply. "Can't you see I have got some ridiculous salesperson selling something or other?"

"I am not selling anything," said the Fat Fairy. "Come on, do you want this wish or not? I am not standing here all day waiting. I have other places to go, other wishes to give."

"What do you mean, a wish?" said Dad.

"Oh dear. It is quite simple. You wish for something. When you've wished for it, I give it to you and I can be on my way," said the Fat Fairy, folding her arms firmly.

"I don't understand," said Dad. "Which company are you from? They should know better than to let you go walking round the streets looking like that, your wings all lopsided and your tiara that looks as if it's been sat on."

"Oh give me strength," said the Fat Fairy. "Have you any notion what I've been through to get here? It's amazing you were given these two wishes. Never known it to happen before in one household."

"Please, Dad, just wish," said Thomas.

"You were here for Thomas's birthday," said Dad, looking puzzled.

"Yes, I gave your son a wish. Now I am back to give you one," said the Fat Fairy.

"I don't need it," said Dad.

"Please, Dad," said Thomas again. He could see the Fat Fairy was on the point of leaving.

"Sorry, I can't hang around, dear," she said.

"Please, please Dad," said Thomas, who now felt quite desperate. "Wish to have fun."

"That's quite enough of this nonsense," said Dad. "Just pull yourself together, young man."

The Fat Fairy turned and started to walk away.

"You've ruined it," said Thomas angrily, "like you ruin everything." He was going back inside when he heard his dad say almost in a whisper, "I wish I could have... fun."

It was too late. The Fat Fairy was too far away to hear. Dad was still standing with the door open when suddenly the Fat Fairy turned round and looked at Dad. She gave a loud belch and said, "All this wishing plays havoc with my insides," and with that she was gone.

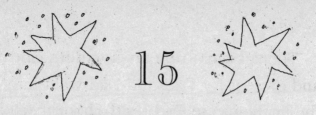

15

Dad closed the front door and started saying "You see, nothing has changed." Then he looked at Thomas as if he had never seen him before and started to laugh and laugh and laugh. Thomas looked at him, worried at first that something had gone really wrong. Then he realised that Dad wasn't laughing a hollow shallow laugh, but a laugh that comes when you are enjoying yourself.

"Oh Thomas, oh Thomas, did you see what I saw? The fattest fairy in the world. Well, it's made my day. Don't think I've laughed like that in ages."

"Yes, Dad," said Thomas, "it's your birthday treat. Happy Birthday!" He gave his dad a big hug.

"What did I do," said Dad, still smiling, "to have such a boy as you?"

Thomas went upstairs to get his card and present for Dad, and Dad went into the kitchen to make breakfast for them both. When he came down Dad was standing there looking at the wall.

"Awfully dull this room is. I never noticed it before," he said.

"Yes," said Thomas. "Mum wanted to paint it full of colour."

"I stopped her," Dad said sadly. "What a fool I've been. Is it too late?"

"No, Dad," said Thomas. He went over to the drawer where Mum kept her scrapbook full of all the paint samples and colours she would like to paint the house. Dad looked at it.

"We'll do it. We will paint it for her just as she wanted," said Dad. "Oh no, we can't! We wouldn't be able to do it in time. She would come back and find ladders up all over the place and that would upset her…"

"Dad," said Thomas, "my friend Mr Vinnie is a painter and decorator."

"I don't know about that. I think I was rather rude to Mr Vinnie," said Dad.

"It doesn't matter," said Thomas. "If I tell him that the Fat Fairy called he will understand."

"Why would he understand?" said Dad.

"Because he was granted a wish when he was my age and he wished to fly," said Thomas.

"Like you. All this time you've flown and like a fool I've pretended not to see. Life is just too dull and ordinary for that kind of magic. But now it's as if a mist has risen. My eyes have sparkles in them."

They had breakfast together. Thomas gave Dad his card and the little box he had painted which Dad said was the best box he had ever had. After breakfast, they called Mr Vinnie who came round straight away. In no time at all Dad, Mr Vinnie, and Thomas had got one room painted. With two flying painters and Dad doing the skirting, it didn't take long.

Dad and Thomas had one of the best days they had ever had together. In the evening they had a takeaway sitting on the kitchen floor, laughing and telling jokes.

Mr Vinnie asked Dad if he remembered any of his magic tricks. Dad did and said he had a few of them still locked in the garden shed. It was just beginning to get dark when they went out, and there along with the box of magic tricks was the covered motorbike. Thomas felt a bit guilty because he knew what it was.

"What's that, Dad?" he said, pointing to the tarpaulin. Dad pulled the cover off and there stood the Harley with its sidecar gleaming in the darkness.

"Well I never," said Mr Vinnie. "What a beauty!"

Dad smiled the broadest smile Thomas had ever seen.

"I used to take Rita out on it. We had a good time together. When Thomas was little we took him as well. We went to the seaside, we went all over the place..." He stopped. "I'd forgotten all the fun we used to have."

"It doesn't matter," said Mr Vinnie. "Why don't we see in the morning if this old thing works?"

"You could go and pick up Mum," said Thomas excitedly.

"Then me and my young flying helper will help finish the painting," said Mr Vinnie.

16

The next morning bright and early, Mr Vinnie turned up with a freshly baked loaf of bread which they ate in large slices, with melted butter. It tasted of white clouds. They filled the bike with petrol and to everyone's amazement it worked first time.

Mr Vinnie lent Dad his flying jacket and goggles. He looked great setting off on the bike, it made the most wonderful putt-putting noise.

Thomas and Mr Vinnie worked fast. They finished the sitting-room and Mum and Dad's bedroom. They laid the table the way Mum liked it with a white tablecloth and a bunch of flowers from

the garden. Mr Vinnie and Thomas felt very pleased with themselves.

By the time Mum came back the whole house shone and smelt of new paint. Mum cried with joy.

"Oh my word! What have you done?"

Dad came in with Mum's suitcase.

"Do you like it?" he said.

Mum turned to look at him. "This was your idea?" she said, amazed.

"Yes, I've been a fool, Rita. For too many years I've wanted to be like everybody else. I never saw what an extraordinary family I have. Being like everybody else means you don't exist. I didn't leave it too late?" he said anxiously.

"No Alan, you haven't left it too late. But what's happened to you?" said Mum.

"Well, I think maybe it's your birthday present," said Dad.

Thomas looked a little baffled. As far as he knew Mum had not given Dad a birthday present.

"The Fat Fairy you sent me," said Dad. "She made me laugh so much."

Mum looked at Thomas and at Mr Vinnie and smiled. "What did you wish for?" she said.

"I wished to have fun," said Dad sheepishly.

"Oh Alan, oh Alan Top, I love you!" said Mum.

17

Dad was quite a different person after that. On Monday he and Mum went to see Mr March the headmaster, who agreed to take Thomas back as long as he kept the flying down. It didn't matter as much to Thomas that some people still refused to see what an amazing thing he could do. The most important people in his life knew, and that was all that mattered.

Dad rearranged Thomas's party and they didn't invite Mr Spoons. "He's jolly good with babies but not for you, my son," said Dad. Instead Mr Vinnie came over to help Thomas to give his friends a little go flying round the garden. Mum made a wonderful tea and Dad did some truly wicked magic tricks. It couldn't have been a greater success. When everybody had gone home Thomas stood in the garden with Dad looking at the sun setting.

"Next time Mr Vinnie comes round we're going to take you up there," said Thomas. Dad laughed. "Then I'll have to cut down on the cream teas," he said, giving Thomas a hug. "Go on with you. I know you want to be off up there, but don't be too long."

"Thanks, Dad," said Thomas.

18

Thomas flew to the park and sat at the top of Alexandra Palace. It was his favourite place up here with the birds. He was thinking how wonderful it was to fly when out of the blue the Fat Fairy landed next to him.

"Hello, Thomas," said the Fat Fairy.

Thomas couldn't believe his luck. "How great to see you again," he said.

"Just popped by to see how you're doing," said the Fat Fairy. "I've been watching this story unfold, dear. It tickled my fancy."

"Do you know all my friends are looking for you?" said Thomas.

"Everybody's looking out for me, dear, but they don't often find me," said the Fat Fairy, smiling.

"I want to thank you for making it all

all right," said Thomas.

"No need. I liked the wish you made about your dad having fun, it touched me, it really did," said the Fat Fairy. "But you can't wish for other people."

"Do you choose who to give wishes to?" asked Thomas.

"No that's not in my power. It's the Chief Fairy's decision and he's an old grouch. Always grumbling, and he doesn't have to do the leg work."

Thomas laughed.

"You should see him. Beats me why he should complain so much. He sleeps most of the time. All he has to do is give me a list of people and off I go. Out in all weathers, I am."

"Do you always go back and check on people?" said Thomas.

"Occasionally I have to go and remind someone what they wished for," said the Fat Fairy.

"Why?" said Thomas.

"Well, gone and forgotten, haven't they," said the Fat Fairy.

Thomas found it hard to believe anyone could forget a wish given by her.

"People grow up and they forget all sorts of things. Like your dad. It had got so bad with him that he had to wish for fun before it could happen."

"It was the best wish ever," said Thomas.

"I thought it would be," said the Fat Fairy.

Thomas looked at her lopsided wings and her tiara glinting in the evening sun, and said, just to make quite sure Mr Vinnie was right, "My wish won't leave me, will it?"

"Oh, bless your cotton socks. No dear, once you've wished for something, you've got it for life, whether you like it or not. That's why, Thomas, you've got to be careful what you wish for."

"I'm very happy with my wish, and so is Dad with his," said Thomas.

"You both should be. You wished for sensible things, things that could happen. Well, I can't sit here all day chatting to you. Must be on my way. Before I go I would like to wish you one thing, though," said the Fat Fairy.

"What's that?" said Thomas.

"I would like to wish you all the best, Thomas Top."